To Catch A Breath

Copyright © 2024 by Larry Griggs

ARPress
45 Dan Road Suite 5
Canton MA 02021

Hotline: 1(888) 821-0229
Fax: 1(508) 545-7580

Ordering Information:

Quantity sales. Special discounts are available on quantity purchases by corporations, associations, and others. For details, contact the publisher at the address above.

Printed in the United States of America.

ISBN-13:   Softcover   979-8-89389-363-2
                eBook   979-8-89389-364-9

Library of Congress Control Number: 2024916632

Table of Contents

Chapter 1

Strange Nights

As I lie in bed staring up at the ceiling, I was experiencing this uncomfortable and eerie feeling centered around all the strange things that had taken place at my uncle's small farm. For as long as I could remember, he and my aunt Alberta had lived on this farm twenty miles outside Winstonville, Arkansas. We rarely visited because as Uncle Elijah would say, "We were city boys, and we didn't know anything about farming," yet they would always visit us there in the city. Now, Aunt Alberta was mysteriously dead, we find out that Uncle Elijah has been being pressured about selling his farm, young Black men have mysteriously started disappearing, and strange sightings in the woods have been reported on the outskirts of the farm. How in the hell am I supposed to sleep with all this shit on my mind? My cousin James and I decided to come down and stay with Uncle Elijah to hopefully help him get through this rough time and lift his spirits, especially with the passing of Aunt Alberta. James, a recent graduate student at a city college here in Detroit, and me, a struggling musician in a blues band, had plenty of time on our hands. With not much really going on for either of us, our parents convinced us to come down and spend quality time with our uncle Elijah. I really wish someone had given us the full story before convincing us to come down for a few weeks. We thought that we would be visiting a grieving farmer, but it turned out to be quite a bit more than that.

Uncle Elijah raised hogs, chickens, and a few cows and was always up early, like four thirty every morning. One night, I heard these loud voices outside near the hog pens. I couldn't make out what was being said, but I could tell that one of the voices was Uncle Elijah's. At breakfast that morning, I decided to ask Uncle Elijah what was he arguing about. He said that it wasn't an argument at all. He said that it was a friend of his that would come by early to help him feed the hogs, and that they had to talk loud over the noises of the hogs. I did not question him any further, even though I could only hear the two men and not the hogs.

We all loved Aunt Alberta and were heartbroken at her passing. She was a very lively and hardworking woman, just like Uncle Elijah.

We were all now worried about our uncle because for so long they were a team, and now, suddenly, she is gone. On the surface, Uncle Elijah seemed fine, but he had to be hurting something awful inside.

I finally realize that I was just not going to get any sleep, so I rolled over out of bed, slipped on my jeans and tennis shoes, and walked down the hallway to James's bedroom. I eased the door open, and just as I thought, James was wide awake. We sat in his room for a few minutes talking about Aunt Alberta and all the other strange happenings centered around this farm, and decided since we were wide awake, we might as well take the conversation to the front porch and not wake Uncle Elijah at two thirty in the morning. James put on his jeans and boots, and to the front porch we quietly crept.

We were both having the same concerns about this place, and that's what we were talking about when we noticed it. A bright orange glow was shining at a distance behind the chicken coop. It was strange. What could this light be? A fire in the middle of the woods? With all the reports of these strange things going on about this farm and the outskirts of it, my curiosity peaked. James looked at me, and I looked at him, and James said, "Nope, I'm not going!" As soon as James finished with his last word, I remembered that it was around this time of night a few nights earlier that I overheard Uncle Elijah and someone arguing near the hog pen. Something in me was telling me that that argument had something to do with this strange light in the distance.

I told James that I wanted to know what this light was all about. James said, "Man, you must be crazy. Let's get out of here." After calming James down, I was able to convince him to follow me toward this light. James really didn't want to go, but he didn't want me going alone either, so he reluctantly followed toward this light in the woods.

The closer we got to the woods, a loud odor became increasingly prevalent. This was an unfamiliar smell, yet it kept getting stronger and stronger the closer we got.

We came upon this opening in the woods and slowly and nervously walked ahead. As we got closer, we saw a gathering of people dressed in dark clothes with hoodies covering their heads. It was too dark, and we were too far away to make out what was really going on. All we could see was this group of the people all marching around this large bonfire. They were constantly throwing things onto the fire and making strange noises. Suddenly, we heard this loud fearful screaming coming from the crowd of people. "Please don't do this, please!" Several people were dragging a young Black guy dressed only in blue jeans, with no shirt or shoes, hurriedly toward the burning fire. As they got him closer toward the fire, I recognized that it was the same young Black guy who had asked me for directions earlier the day before. The way he was screaming was terrifying. Suddenly, I felt this grip on my right arm pulling me; it was James. "Let's go, man!" James shouted. As we turned to run, we both stumble over this wire with cans attached to it making a loud noise.

We hurriedly got back to our feet, but we could hear the crowd yelling, "There they are, let's get them!" We began running. We were running with the fear of death in us. We were running with so much fear until it was hard to catch a breath.

Chapter 2

Shots Fired

Somehow, we were able to make it to the break of the woods, and could see Uncle Elijah's house in the distance. Behind us, we could hear people yelling and dogs barking like we were runaway slaves. As we got closer to the house, they got closer to us. Then suddenly, the sound of a shotgun blast silenced the air as we fell at our uncle's feet on his porch, with a double barrel shotgun in his hands. He fired a second shot, and we could still hear the dogs barking, but they were going in the other direction. "Get in the house!" Elijah yelled. That's exactly what we did.

As we sat motionless in the living room, all the nightmarish sounds were finally gone. "You boys should have never left this house, especially in the middle of the night!" Elijah angrily said. Those were the only words spoken for the rest of the night.

Early the next morning, Elijah was making breakfast, and James and I were still sitting up in my bedroom, not having even considered trying to sleep. I got up and walked into the kitchen. Without saying good morning or anything like it, I calmly asked Elijah, "What was that all about last night?" Uncle Elijah said, "You boys could have been hurt."

I responded by saying, "I believe a young Black man was killed in those woods last night! He was screaming for his life while those people were dragging him toward that fire." I got louder and yelled, "What in the world is going on here?"

"It's none of your business!" Elijah shouted.

"How is it that burning Black people to death is not my business?" I retorted.

"You don't know that that happened," Elijah said. "We saw them dragging him to the fire!" I yelled.

"Did you see them put him into the fire?" asked Elijah.

"No, that's when we got tangled up in those cans," I remembered.

Chapter 3

The Art of the Steal

"They know you are here. You and James are going to have to leave." Just then, James walked into the room. "We are going to have to leave? That's not something you have to tell me twice!" James yelled. "Larry, let's go! Let's go!" James kept shouting.

"Wait a minute, James, Uncle Elijah has some explaining to do," I said. I turned to Uncle Elijah and with a stern voice said, "We are not going anywhere until you tell us what's going on around here!"

Uncle Elijah walked out of the kitchen and sat down in the living room with his head bowed and his hands clasped between his knees. It was several minutes before he looked up and said, "I don't want you boys getting involved!"

"Getting involved in what?" I asked.

He suddenly broke down and started screaming, "They killed my Alberta. They killed her!" The next hour and a half, James and I sat and listened to Uncle Elijah tell us what was going on. He said that for the past three years, there had been a concerted effort by a group of townspeople trying to force him to sell his farm. "Some of the offers were outrageously high. I just didn't want to sell." He talked about the fact that he owned the farm outright. No liens or bank holdings, yet several bankers kept visiting, wanting him to sell. "There were many times that lawyers came out, without me seeking them, trying to show me the value in selling the farm, but I always declined. The last guy told me that I would live to regret not selling. There was this big white guy that I saw early one morning near the hog pen calling me outside. I went out with my shotgun thinking that this would scare him away, but he just stood there. I asked him what was it that he wanted. He started saying that there were some powerful people who thought he should sell this farm because it was holding up progress. We began arguing, and finally with me telling him that I was not selling my farm for any amount of money. He left, but not before he told me that he would be back to see whether I had changed my mind. He did come back, but the answer was always the same." I thought to myself that this had to be who I heard him arguing with early that morning when he said that it was just a friend, and they had to talk loud over the hogs. "Several months after my last declination, things started happening."

"Things like what?" I asked.

"Well, things started happening late at night when Alberta and I would be awakened with these loud and strange noises. Yet when I would go outside with my shotgun, I never saw anything. Then the cows started getting out through opened fences. Then the hogs would be out. Problems started occurring that had never happened before. Then that one night these noises got so loud outside until Alberta and I both got up. The noise was coming from near the hog pen. I got the shotgun, and Alberta followed behind me. It was extremely dark out this night and the hogs were squealing loudly. As we got closer to the pen, then out of the darkness this voice yelled, "Hey, old man!" Right then, I was hit in the face with what felt like a hard piece of wood. I was knocked out cold. When I woke up hours later, Alberta was lying next to me, and she wasn't breathing. She was dead! The sheriff's office and an ambulance came out, and sure enough my Alberta was gone. The paramedics worked on her, but never got a pulse. The coroner showed up and pronounced her dead. They took Alberta away. They kept asking a bunch of questions about what happened. I tried to explain to them what happened, but they kept looking at me as if I was crazy. In the end, the sheriff's office concluded that me and Alberta came outside late that night, I stepped on the blade of a shovel that was laying on the ground in the darkness, the shovel popped up, hitting me in the head knocking me out. The sheriff said that apparently, Alberta was so upset and scared until she had a heart attack. That's exactly what the coroner ruled as her cause of death, a massive heart attack. Alberta had no other relatives, and it was always her desire to be buried in the cemetery just a couple of miles up the road. We had visited her grave several times since we were here. About a month after the services, the sheriff and two other white men paid me a visit. One said he was a banker, and the other said he was a geo something. I didn't quite understand him. They said that they were just checking on me, yet in the same sentence the sheriff said that it just didn't make any sense for an old man like me to be living out here by myself, and that maybe this would be the right time to sell. He said that the gentleman is prepared to make me a handsome offer that could make me a wealthy man. I told them that Alberta loved this place, and I would never consider selling my farm.

The sheriff and I stood talking while the other men walked around the farm. They soon returned to where we were and got back into the sheriff's car. Before they drove off, the sheriff rolled down his window and said, "Hope this isn't a decision that you will regret!" As they drove off and the dust billowed up behind the car, I started wondering what really happened to Alberta. The more I thought about his words the more my heart began to race. It raced so hard until it was hard for me to catch a breath.

Chpater 4

A Wrench in the Works

James and I had agreed that we would stay a little while longer to help our uncle Elijah out around the farm and to get a better understanding of what really happened that night Aunt Alberta died.

Later that same evening, we began telling Uncle Elijah more about what we had seen in the woods. We told him again about the young shirtless Black man being led, kicking and screaming toward the huge fire by people dressed in black with hoodies covering their faces. We explained to him just how shocking and frightening this was, and that this was the kind of stuff we had only seen in the movies. The most frightening of all of course was when the crowd saw us. Elijah explained that he had seen the same kind of fire about a month earlier and had reported it to the sheriff's department. They came out the next day and said to me that they did see where a small fire had been set, but it looked like it was just a small fire set by raccoon hunters to keep warm. It wasn't unusual for people to hunt raccoons at night, so I thought little of it. Things settled down after that, and everything got quiet around the farm, but it was still eerie. Someone had to be opening those fences and pens letting those animals out. I needed to know who. It was clear that somebody wanted Elijah's farm badly, but why? Somebody wanted to make things so bad for an old man to run this farm by himself until he would have to sell. Now James and I are here. Simply by us being here must have thrown a wrench into the works.

Chapter 5

A Dirty Hog

Early the next morning, we were all sitting on th front porch when James asked, "Why did the bankers want to buy the farm so badly?"

Elijah said, "All they ever told me was that some investors wanted to build some sort of factory, and that this would be the ideal site."

"Some kind of factory?" I wondered. "In a farming community like this?" Later that day, James and I were out near the hog pens just talking about some of the things Uncle Elijah had told us, when we noticed that several hogs were all rooting in the same spot. We initially thought that they had killed something and were trying to eat it. We decided to sooeythem away to get a better look as to what was going on. As one of the hogs began to move away, we noticed that its snout was all black and shiny. As the rest moved away, they all were covered in this black substance. James ran to the barn, retrieved a shovel, and began digging in the same spot the hogs were rooting. The more he dug, the more this black liquid billowed up. By this time, Elijah had made his way to the pen. "What you boys doing in that hog pen?" Elijah yelled. James stepped aside to allow Elijah to see where he was digging. "That's oil!" Elijah said. Oil it was. Suddenly, the pieces began coming together. Why all the interest by so many people? The sheriff, the bankers, the real estate people, this guy that came out with sheriff and the banker, it was all just a ploy to get our uncle to sell this place for this oil underneath it. This was incredible. We couldn't believe what we were seeing. It was so shocking!

The next few weeks became very hectic, and at the same time extremely strange. Black folks who were considered missing began showing up. The young Black guy whom we thought was being burned to death that night, showed up working for the same real estate agency that was trying to get Uncle Elijah to sell his farm. Even the sheriff started acting funny after Elijah was able to bring the FBI in to further investigate the death of Aunt Alberta. The coroner left town for a while, but later returned.

The farm was now covered with oil people. Geologists and geophysicists from all over the country were brought in to examine the oil bed that was determined to be smack in the middle of Uncle Elijah's farm. This was wonderful news, yet sad because Aunt Alberta had to die never knowing why. People whom Uncle Elijah had considered close friends were all involved in this elaborate scheme to basically steal his farm that he never knew was sitting on black gold. It was hard to comprehend. When you really think about the magnitude of it all it becomes hard to catch a breath.

Things began to change a lot, especially around the farm. The difference this time is that there was no conniving and pretending. Elijah Williams and his black gold mine was the talk of the town and the surrounding areas. The pigs, chickens, and cows were all replaced with gigantic drilling machines, excavators, and other dirt moving machines. The lawyers were all on Uncle Elijah's team this time. Mom and Dad had come down from the city, and everything was happening so fast. Elijah was on the verge of becoming a multimillionaire. Everything was good except for one thing: Elijah was sad and miserable. This was not who he was, and most of all, the love of his life was no longer by his side. Even though Elijah was becoming a millionaire, he also was becoming a very depressed and angry man. He never slept, and he had declared that no matter what became of his farm, the home that he and his beloved Alberta shared wasn't going anywhere!

Chapter 6

The Top Blows

Time moved on, and the farm began to change into a sprawling magnate, turning Uncle Elijah into a multimillionaire. Buildings began popping up, people were everywhere, yet in the center of all of that was this small three- bedroom wooden structure that housed this seventy-five-year-old broken Black man. He was broken, but he was slowly becoming angrier and angrier. The wealthier he got, the angrier he got. Then one day, he came out on the porch of this small house dwarfed by all these big buildings, and all you could hear were shotgun blasts all around. Uncle Elijah was letting them loose. He was constantly reloading and blasting in the air. People were scattered all over the place when the sheriff deputies finally showed up. When they were finally able to bring him out, he was crying like a baby and yelling that he wanted everybody off his property, and that's exactly what happened, including himself.

Elijah was charged with discharging a firearm in public, along with several other misdemeanors. When we finally were able to bail him out, he kept screaming that someone needs to pay for the death of Alberta. It was hard to see this once proud and stout man now seemingly crumbling before our eyes.

Chapter 7

Dreams

After a few days, things resumed back to what you could consider normal, except now Elijah never came out of the house. He said that Alberta came to him in a dream saying that someone needs to pay, and that he needs to make sure they do.

He remembered the coroner had ruled that Alberta died from a heart attack. Elijah wanted an investigation started into how his beloved wife had passed away. By this time, there were no more animals around what used to be the farm because of all the drilling and new construction. James and I had gotten an apartment in town that our uncle Elijah was paying for. We couldn't live with Elijah anymore, frankly because he wanted us out! One day, I got a call from Elijah wanting me and James to ride into town with him. We came over, and he was already sitting in his old Chevrolet pickup waiting on us. I got in the front and James got in the back. We spoke and I said, "Where are we headed, Unc?" He didn't answer, so I shut up and just rode. We drove past the coroner's office about a block and a half, and Elijah pulled over.

He said, "I want you boys to walk back to the coroner's office, and go in and wait for me." He said that he would come in behind us, but he didn't want anyone to know that we were together. Most of all, when he leaves, we should stay and say that we were looking for a summer job. We got up, walked back to the coroner's office, and sat down in the waiting room. Before anyone could address us, Uncle Elijah walked in. He walked straight to the receptionist and asked to speak with the coroner. They recognized him right away, and soon the coroner was out speaking to him. The conversation got heated. I had never heard Uncle Elijah curse before, but he sounded like he had done it before. It seemed as if they were going to trade blows, but the coroner threatened to call the police. Uncle Elijah had shaken this guy up until he was as red as he could be. We just sat there as Elijah left the office. When he left, the coroner leaned over the counter and said, "If only this old bastard knew the truth, I would be in deep shit!" He pulled himself together and began to walk back to the back, and that's when he noticed us sitting there. "What can I help you boys with?" Just as instructed, we said that we were looking for a summer job. Still being upset, he yelled at us, saying, "We are not hiring!" We jumped up and ran up the street where Uncle Elijah was waiting. Before we could close the door to the car, Elijah said, "What did that son of a bitch say?"

We told him exactly what we heard.

When he heard what the coroner said, he said, "That's just what she said he would say."

We were confused, so James asked Elijah, "Who said that he would say that?"

Elijah turned to us with tears in his eyes and said, "Alberta told me, Alberta told me!" What Uncle Elijah said was so shocking until it was hard for me to catch a breath!

Chapter 8

The Heat Is On

Elijah dropped us back off at the apartment, and we assumed that he went back home. About an hour later, there was this knock on the door, and there was Uncle Elijah standing there with this old white guy whom we had never seen before. We invited them into the apartment, and Elijah introduced him as Attorney Steinbeck. Uncle Elijah said that Mr. Steinbeck had a few questions that he would like to ask us. The first question he asked was, "What did you boys hear the coroner say about your uncle when Elijah left his office?" We told him exactly what we heard. Mr. Steinbeck turned to Elijah and said, "Are you sure that you are willing to go through with this?" Elijah said, "Hell yeah, I'm willing to go through with this. These sons of bitches had something to do with Alberta's death, and I want to know what really happened to my wife and what role whoever played in her death!"

Mr. Steinbeck said, "Alright, I will call you later today, and we will talk about how we will proceed from here." He got up and walked out of the door. Elijah told us to come by his house at around 6:00 p.m. this evening, and he would fill us in on what's going on.

James and I got to Uncle Elijah house at around five thirty that evening. That was long as we could wait. When we got there, several men were just coming out of Elijah's house. We waited a few minutes, then we rushed into the house. Uncle Elijah was sitting at the kitchen table with a bunch of papers scattered across it. "What's going on, Uncle?" I hurriedly asked.

"Sit down at the table, and I will tell you what's going on," Elijah responded. "I've been talking with Alberta! She is telling me that a heart attack is not why she is dead!"

I looked at James, and he was already looking at me. "Auntie Alberta is dead and buried, how can you be talking to her?" I asked.

"She is coming to me in my dreams and telling me that the coroner and the sheriff are behind it all! The men that just left here are FBI investigators, and they are working on the case. Nobody would listen to me when I was just a small-time chicken and pig farmer, but now, I am a wealthy oil man. Now they are listening! That's what the coroner meant when we were at his office and he was saying if only you knew the truth! I thought out loud, tomorrow morning, we are going to exhume Alberta's body and have a private autopsy done on her," Elijah said quietly.

"Are you serious?" I asked.

"As a heart attack!" Elijah responded. "That's what she wants me to do! She keeps telling me to find the truth," Elijah continued. After hearing those words coming from Uncle Elijah's mouth, my heart started pumping faster and faster, so fast until it became hard for me to catch a breath.

Chapter 9

The Exhumation

Early the next morning, we all rode to the cemetery where Aunt Alberta was buried. When we got there, a backhoe, a contraption used to extract the casket from the grave, and a box truck were already next to her gravesite. The sheriff's office pulled up shortly after we arrived, and several other people, including those who were at Elijah's house the day before, pulled up a few minutes later.

Soon the casket was exhumed and loaded onto the box truck. There was a brief conversation between the men driving the truck and the men who met with Elijah the day before, and then the truck drove away. James and I huddled up with Elijah and asked him what was happening next. Elijah said that a private medical examiner had been hired to do a second autopsy on Alberta, and as soon as that was done, they would call him with the results.

Several days later, Uncle Elijah called us over to his house and told us that the medical examiner detected a combination of morphine and codeine in Aunt Alberta's bones. I said, "What does that mean?"

Elijah said to us, "Your Aunt Alberta was murdered!"

That statement was hard to hear. "Why would anyone want to harm Aunt Alberta?" I asked. "What could be gained by her death?" Those were questions that were circling in my head. Elijah told us that the only thing that could be gained was the black gold that was buried underneath our farm. He said that somebody figured if she were out of the way, there would be no way that he would stay on that farm alone. Somebody figured that he would soon sell his farm, not knowing that he would be selling the oil at the same time.

Elijah told us that he had hired a group of lawyers to get to the bottom of all of this and that they told him that they plan to follow the trails from all that has taken place, and if it leads to the sheriff and the coroner, then so be it.

Chapter 10

The Truth Will Set You Free

The medical examiner had convinced Elijah that Alberta did not die from a heart attack as the sheriff and coroner had said but from a combination of those drugs that had somehow been injected into her body.

The next day, a lawsuit was filed, and an investigation was begun into the death of Alberta Williams, naming the Winston County sheriff's department and the county's coroner's office as defendants in the suit. The FBI soon began an investigation into the goings-on of the sheriff's department and the coroner's office, as it related to the death of Aunt Alberta. News reporters were all over the place and the town was abuzz. What a way to spend the Summer!

The story of Elijah Williams and his deceased wife, Alberta, was all over the local and state news. The investigation into the sheriff's department and coroner's office made national news. This little town, once quiet and peaceful, wasn't so quiet and peaceful anymore.

As time went on, James and I decided that we were going to continue to stay here to be with Elijah for as long as necessary. We weren't aware at the time, but we would play an integral part in the actions that were about to take place.

Chapter 11

The Trial

Several weeks went by, and James and I received subpoenas ordering us to be a party to the upcoming trial. As I began to spend more time with Uncle Elijah, I began to see him in a way that I had never seen him before. It was as if he had a newfound energy and calmness about him. He was focused and serious, more so than ever before. I had a chance to talk to Uncle Elijah right before the trial started. I mentioned to him that I had seen this new energy in him and sharpness. He said to me, "It's not me alone, Alberta has given me this strength to do right by her!" It was at that point that I started to believe that.

The first day of the trial was unreal. Elijah's lawyers were the best I had ever seen. James and I sat right behind Elijah on the first day, and it was then that James made a startling revelation. He said that he wondered what kind of lawyers and even what kind of case this would be if Elijah wasn't wealthy now from the oil on his land. He said there probably wouldn't even be a trial. Money opens doors. I hadn't even thought of that until just that very moment.

The first person to take the stand was a geologist whom Uncle Elijah recognized as having come to the farm with the sheriff. He testified that several years ago, his office had drones flying over the county searching for water plains. He further testified that one of the drones detected what appeared to be a possible oil well around Elijah Williams's farm. He went on to say that he later spoke with the sheriff about making Mr. Williams aware of the possibility of his farm sitting on an oil well, but the sheriff suggested that they should make sure that there was indeed oil there before anything was said to Elijah. He also said that he and the sheriff went to the farm on several occasions to use instruments to make sure that there was, indeed, oil on and around the farm. The instruments indicated that there was oil underneath 90 percent of the farm. The geologist went on to say that the sheriff convinced him not to mention his findings to Mr. Williams just yet, so he never did.

I was called to take the stand after the geologist. I told of how James and I went wandering into the woods because of a bright light that we had seen not too far in the distance from Uncle Elijah's farm. I told of seeing lots of people dressed in dark clothes gathering around a large fire. All were wearing hoodies. I told how James and I had seen a young Black man seemingly being ushered toward the fire, kicking and screaming. I told of us tripping over cans that caused the crowd to see us and chase us back to the farm, and of Elijah firing off his shotgun to scare the crowd away.

As the trial went on, everything that Uncle Elijah had told us about what had been happening started to come to light. It seemed that the list of people who knew about the oil on Elijah's farm kept growing. The next witness to take the stand was the young Black guy who we thought was about to be thrown onto the burning fire that night we ventured into the woods. He told the story of how he was hired by a local realtor to play a role in what he thought was some sort of play. He said that he was only trying to make some money. After his testimony then, of course, the realtor was called to the stand. That was when the shit hit the fan! The realtor said that he had been informed by the sheriff more than a year ago that Elijah's farm was sitting right in the middle of an oil bed. He said that the sheriff told him that they needed to find a way to get that old man to sell that farm before he found out about the oil. He said he was only trying to convince Elijah to sell the farm, and that it was the sheriff's idea. He said the sheriff said that they all could stand to benefit from him selling that farm. After several months of unsuccessfully trying to convince Elijah to sell the farm, the sheriff suggested that they try to scare him into selling. He said that he did employ some people to try to spook Elijah several nights, but he never intended for anyone to get hurt. He said that he was shocked when he heard the news that Alberta was dead.

There was another person called to the stand that to this point, was a surprise to everyone in the court. The thing that made him so unique was that he was led into the courtroom in shackles, not by the sheriff's deputies, but by the FBI investigators. He testified that, on the night of Alberta's death, he did lure Elijah and his wife out of the house early the morning she died. He said that he surprised Elijah by hitting him in the face with the wooden handle of a shovel because he knew that Elijah was going to have his shotgun. He said that the old lady tried to fight him, and all he remembers is that the sheriff and the coroner showed up to pull her away from him. According to him, the sheriff had paid him $200 to do what he did on that night, and $100 on other times he had gone the farm to spook Elijah. He said that when he left the farm, the old man was unconscious and breathing, and the sheriff and the coroner had the old lady restrained. He didn't know anything about what happened to the old lady, but he never did anything to hurt her.

The banker, who was called next, testified that he did know of the plot to get Mr. Williams to sell his farm but only went to the farm with the sheriff because he asked him to go. He was on the stand only a short time.

The private medical examiner was called next and reported that, after exhumation of Alberta Williams body and doing a second autopsy, there were large amounts of morphine and codeine found in her bones. He said that the amount found in her bones would suggest that her cause of death was homicide. A gasp went across the courtroom. After a few more witnesses had taken the stand, Uncle Elijah's lawyer recalled the man who had hit Uncle Elijah in the face with a shovel, back to the witness stand.

There was only one question asked of this man once he had returned to the stand. The lead attorney asked, "Who was at the farm when you left?"

He said, "Elijah Williams, as I said, was still unconscious, Alberta Williams, Coroner Hugh Joseph, and Sheriff Roger Carwin!" After that statement, the crowded courtroom went into a frenzy! "Order in the court! Order in the court!" the judge yelled as he slammed his gavel down several times!

Since it was late in the evening by this time, the Judge decided to recess until 9:00 a.m. the next day.

Cameras were all over the outside of the courtroom when we exited the building. Elijah was surrounded by his team of lawyers who wouldn't allow him to speak to the media at all.

Chapter 12

Who has the Power

James and I spent the night with Uncle Elijah mainly because he had security surrounding his house and the fact that we didn't want to be bombarded by the press ourselves.

Several of Uncle Elijah's attorneys were there most of the night as well. The conversation on this night was all about the alliance between the sheriff and the coroner. The attorneys were discussing how to get the sheriff arrested. According to Arkansas state law, the only person in the county who can arrest the sheriff in the county would be the county coroner. Since the coroner and the sheriff seemingly were in cahoots in this alleged crime, how can they both be arrested? After doing quite a bit of research, it was concluded that the attorney general was the chief law enforcement officer of the state. So, because of what was heard in testimony, it seemed as if the next step would be to start preparing to file charges against the sheriff and see how things would shake out with the coroner for the death of Alberta Williams.

Chapter 13

Plan Gone Wrong

The trial resumed promptly at 9:00 a.m. the next morning, and of course, the first person to be called to the witness stand was Sheriff Carwin. Surprisingly, the sheriff admitted to concocting the scheme to get Uncle Elijah to sell his farm. He also admitted to paying the guy that knocked Elijah out.

Elijah's attorney asked him what happened at the farm when only he and the coroner were left there with Alberta Williams while Elijah was unconscious. He said that Hugh suggested that she be sedated because she was continually trying to fight and was screaming about her husband lying on the ground. Hugh said, "I'm going to have to sedate her to calm her down!"

"After Hugh sedated her, we agreed that we would stay there until she woke up and tell her that I was just out patrolling, and Hugh was riding with me when we saw all the commotion. We were going to say to Alberta that we saw Elijah on the ground, and she was fighting with the man who had knocked him out. The only problem was that she never woke up. We stayed there several minutes trying to revive her, but she wasn't breathing and there was no heartbeat. She was dead. Hugh had somehow injected her with the wrong syringe, killing Alberta. We never planned on killing anybody. We just wanted the old man to sell. He never would have gotten the kind of offers from anybody like the ones offered to him by us."

The attorney asked, "Who do you mean when you say us?"

"I mean Jack Phillips at the bank!" At that time, the banker got up and attempted to leave the courtroom, but the judge ordered him to sit back down. As soon as the banker was seated, the judge beckoned for men to come into the courtroom. Two men from the attorney general's office came into the courtroom and escorted the sheriff out of the room. The judge then instructed Elijah's attorney to call his next witness. Of course, everybody in the courtroom knew who that was going to be. The attorney turned to the judge and said, "I call to the witness stand Jack Phillips, president of the Winstonville Bank and Trust."

The banker nervously came to the witness stand. The attorney asked the banker about his relationship with the sheriff as it was related to the offers made to the Elijah Williams. Mr. Phillips immediately threw the sheriff under the bus. "It was Roger's idea to offer him the money," the banker yelled out. The attorney asked Mr. Phillips if there ever was an appraisal done on Mr. Williams's farm prior to it being known that oil was on the property. Mr. Phillips said, "Yes!"

"What was it appraised for?" the attorney asked. "Roughly eighty to ninety thousand," said the banker.

"What was the highest offer you made to Mr. Williams?" asked the attorney.

The banker turned to the judge and said, "Two hundred and fifty thousand!"

"How much would the farm be worth today?" The banker bowed his head and said, "Millions!"

The banker soon left the witness stand and the last witness for the day was Hugh Joseph, the coroner for the county. Before the attorney could ask Mr. Joseph one question, he started yelling, "It was an accident! It was dark, and I mistakenly injected her with the wrong syringe. It was simply an accident that went terribly wrong!" The attorney asked Mr. Joseph to calm down and let him ask the questions. The first question asked of Mr. Joseph was, "What about Mr. Williams lying on the ground, was any attention given to him at all?"

"We could hear him snoring, so we figured that he was knocked unconscious," replied the coroner.

"Why was it necessary to sedate Mrs. Williams?" asked the attorney. "Because she was so hysterical, we just didn't want the old lady to have a heart attack!" the coroner replied.

"How ironic," replied the attorney. "What did you rule as the cause of death for Mrs. Williams?" whipped the attorney.

The coroner bowed his head and almost inaudibly replied, "Heart attack." "Can you repeat that loud enough where you can be heard by everyone?" He then yelled out loud, "Heart attack!"

"So you knew all along that you had killed Mrs. Williams, yet you recorded her death as a heart attack?" asked the attorney. Mr. Joseph mumbled an inaudible sound, and then the attorney slammed his fist on the witness stand and yelled, "I asked you a question, Mr. Joseph!"

Mr. Joseph was startled, but began yelling, "Yes, yes, yes, that's what I recorded it as, a heart attack!" The audience began to mumbling among themselves and the judge hit his gavel again, ordering order in the courtroom.

The judge asked if there were any more questions of this person, and the attorneys replied, "No." It was then that the judge beckoned for the attorney general's office to come in and remove the coroner. That ended court for that evening.

That night, things were buzzing. Telephone calls were coming in from all over town, reporting things they knew about the plot to steal Uncle Elijah's farm. Most importantly, two phone calls were made to Elijah's attorneys informing them that Sheriff Carwin and coroner Joseph had agreed to plead guilty to a plea bargain, admitting to causing the death of Alberta Williams. That was all Elijah really wanted out of this whole ordeal. He felt satisfaction in a confusing kind of way. Had he not adhered to what was coming to him in his dream, the real cause of the death of his beloved wife, Alberta, might not have ever been known. The conspiracy committed toward him to steal his farm and the oil beneath it by basically an entire town may not have ever come to light.

Elijah had become one of the wealthiest men in the entire state of Arkansas, but would gladly give it all away to have his life partner back by his side. The sheriff and the coroner received huge prison sentences. Several of the other players in this tragedy are also spending time behind bars for their parts in the whole ordeal. Uncle Elijah has a lot of older females that he is having to fend off almost daily, but emotionally he seems to be doing better every day. As for James and me, we went back home with a lot more than we came down with. As we think about all that we went through, in just one Summer, it makes the thought of it all hard to catch a breath.

About the Author

Born in the Mississippi Delta in the late 1950s, the third of eight children and being blessed with a creative mind, Larry loved writing. His first love was poetry. Eventually deciding to put his creative gifts to first his memoir (I Dreamed That I Lived) and now fiction. Now in retirement, he has plenty of time to focus on that which has always been the one thing that has allowed him to express his thoughts in a way that hopefully will bring enjoyment to all those who may have an opportunity to read his works. This story is one that has been stored away in his mind and now has surfaced to allow the world to see. Enjoy, there is much more to come.v

www.ingramcontent.com/pod-product-compliance
Lightning Source LLC
Chambersburg PA
CBHW040914010826

48978CB00013BB/1294